The Pig Scramble

WRITTEN BY **Jessica Kinney**
ILLUSTRATED BY **Sarah S. Brannen**

published by

Islandport Press
P.O. Box 10
267 U.S. Route One, Suite B
Yarmouth, Maine 04096
www.islandportpress.com

ISBN: 978-1-934031-61-2
Library of Congress Control Number: 2011925634
Printed by Everbest Printing Co. Ltd, Guangzhou, China
Production Date: May 9, 2011
Job/Batch # 101379

ISLANDPORT PRESS   Yarmouth • Maine

For Reid, who made, and makes,
it all possible
                    —jessica kinney

To my sister Jennie, for a lifetime
of support and encouragement
                    —sarah s. brannen

The Pig Scramble

WRITTEN BY Jessica Kinney

ILLUSTRATED BY Sarah S. Brannen

Clarence, an imaginative and curious little boy, lived on a small farm with lots of cows, his mom, dad, and two big brothers, Robby and Ricky. His brothers were bigger because they were older, but also because they were just BIG.

Clarence always felt small and ordinary next to Robby and Ricky. Robby and Ricky could do almost anything, especially when they helped their father with the farm's many chores. Clarence tried enthusiastically to help, but he didn't end up being very helpful.

When a stubborn calf needed to be moved to another part of the barn, Robby and Ricky wrapped their enormous arms all the way around the baby cow, and lifted the creature just as easily as they could lift Clarence. Clarence, trying to help, would politely ask a calf to move, and get only a rough lick from the calf's pink tongue in reply.

After the cows were milked, Robby and Ricky could carry two metal pails full of milk all the way across the barn to the milk tank without spilling a drop. Clarence couldn't carry a pail from cow to cow without making some kind of mess.

The cats loved it when Clarence worked in the barn.

When it came time to clean out the barn, Robby and Ricky could shovel manure all afternoon (literally, until the cows came home) without breaking much of a sweat. It was smelly work, but it was BIG BOY work.

Clarence, though, could only sweep away the dust his big brothers left behind. Even then, his boots weren't nearly as dirty and smelly as his brothers.

Maybe being the littlest wasn't all bad.

Still, Clarence felt he would never be as big as his brothers. He would always be the little boy who had to stay out of the way.

But not every little boy has an Uncle Leon.

Uncle Leon lived next door to Clarence's family. He was the youngest in a family of five boys. He understood a thing or two about life as the littlest boy in a big family.

The best part of Clarence's day was visiting Uncle Leon in his workshop, which was filled with gadgets and gizmos, spark plugs and screwdrivers, radios and ripsaws. Leon's hands, with wrinkles and veins that reminded Clarence of rivers and canyons, could take apart and put back together any contraption. He could fix anything, from an egg timer to an airplane.

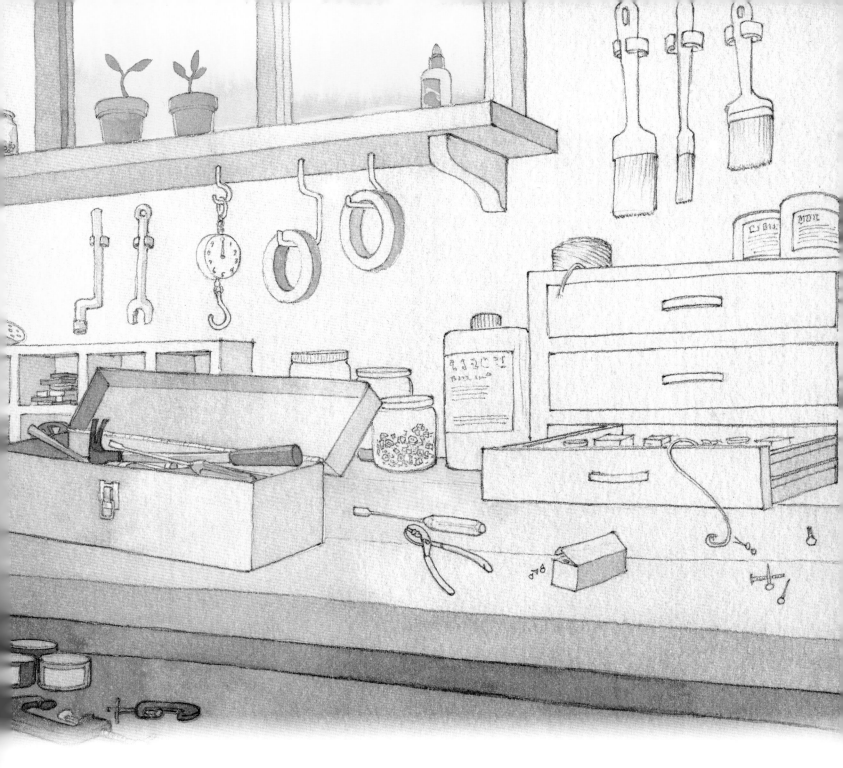

Clarence believed that Uncle Leon could work magic.

Once, after Robby accidentally ran over Clarence's favorite toy truck with the lawnmower, Leon took the twisted and tattered wreck into his workshop. Before Clarence's teary eyes, he transformed the ruins into a better-than-new truck. It even had a bright red paint job and beeped when Clarence moved it in reverse.

And last fall, Leon flew his airplane over a field full of black and white cows. With one wiggle of the plane's wings, he made the cows moo the tune "Mary Had a Little Lamb."

At least, that's what it sounded like to Clarence.

In all the time Clarence spent in Uncle Leon's workshop, though, there was one thing they never talked about: the lone picture on the workshop windowsill. It was a picture of a perfectly plump pig, wearing a necklace with the name "Geraldine" on it. Clarence said a silent hello to Geraldine every time he visited the workshop. Her serene, smiling snout seemed to greet him in turn. Sometimes, Clarence would notice Uncle Leon smiling fondly at Geraldine's picture, too.

Every summer, toward the end of August, when the harvest was in full swing and the air hinted at the coming autumn, Clarence would start to get excited, for it meant just one thing – the County Fair. For little boys on a farm, there isn't anything much more exciting than riding the Ferris wheel and eating salty French fries drenched in vinegar followed by a piping-hot doughboy dusted with powdered sugar.

The chance to eat sweet and salty treats wasn't Clarence's only reason for wanting to go to the fair. No, he had a much more important reason: THE PIG SCRAMBLE.

The pig scramble meant ten children running around a pen chasing a little pig, trying to catch the slippery, squirmy squealer with nothing but their bare hands. The pig did all it could do to avoid being caught, and the children did all they could do to catch it. Whichever child caught the pig got to take it home, which was better than any souvenir the fair had to offer.

Robby and Ricky both had been in pig scrambles when they were Clarence's age, but despite valiant, muddy efforts, neither boy had ever caught a pig. This year, Robby and Ricky were too old for the scramble. This year, it was Clarence's turn.

The day of the scramble, Uncle Leon picked up Clarence and his brothers and drove them to the fair in his restored antique car, which he brought out of the garage on special occasions. It was a treat to sit in the front seat and putter down the road with Uncle Leon.

At the fair, Robby and
Ricky wished Clarence good
luck and then went to help their friends at the
tractor pull. "It's just as well," Clarence thought.
"I'd be even more nervous with them watching me."

Uncle Leon walked with Clarence, past the livestock hall, past the merry-go-round, and past the fried dough to the pigpen where a large group of noisy children had already gathered, eager to catch a pig. Clarence looked around at all the bigger boys (and some girls). He began to sweat, and not just because he'd worn one of Ricky's old flannel shirts. Clarence hoped the fabric and long sleeves would give him some extra grip.

"What's going on in that noggin' of yours?" Uncle Leon asked, with that half-smile he seemed to have on his lips at all times.

Clarence looked up at him with an embarrassed grin. He wasn't sure his little-boy arms could grab and hold on to a pig. "I'm nervous, Uncle Leon," he admitted.

"Well, of course you are!" Leon said loudly, as he patted Clarence's shoulder. Then he gave a bark of a laugh. "But, think of this: if YOU are this nervous, how do you think the PIG feels?"

Somehow, Uncle Leon's words didn't make Clarence feel any better.

As the announcer squawked into the microphone saying all children needed to step up to the gate and wait behind the line, Uncle Leon

scooched down, eye-level with Clarence. He spoke softly, and Clarence had to concentrate to hear him because the kids were screaming with excitement and the pig was squealing, ready to run.

"Clarence, I have two pieces of advice, so listen carefully. One: just before the scramble starts, spit on your hands and rub 'em in the dirt at the edge of the pen. The grittier and dirtier your hands are, the easier it'll be to hold onto that pig. Remember, spit first and THEN rub because the dirt won't stick if you don't."

Clarence was delighted. His mother was forever telling him to wash his hands and now, here was Uncle Leon ordering him not only to SPIT on his hands, but also to rub them in the DIRT.

"The second piece of advice is," and here, Leon paused with that knowing grin and twinkling eye, "let the pig come to you."

And with that, Uncle Leon gently pushed Clarence inside the pen with the other children.

Clarence wasn't sure what to do, so he stood there behind the group, thinking. How could he let a pig come to him? Or let a pig do anything, for that matter?

The announcer began to count: "5...4...3...2..." When he got to "1" the farmer set the pig down at the opposite end of the pen, stepped back outside the gate, and the kids started running.

Clarence stood, staring.
The pig jumped, squealed,
and started to run.

Clarence watched, still, as the mass of children screamed, fell, got up, fell again, and chased that pig all around one end of the pen. Some of the bigger boys (and some girls) almost caught the pig, but it squiggled away just in time, and those kids caught only mouthfuls of mud.

Just as the crowd of kids started to turn around and head back towards where the scramble had started, Clarence realized they were forcing the pig to run right towards him. With no time to waste, Clarence spit on his hands, rubbed them in the dirt, and, well… he let the pig come to him.

Clarence crouched close to the ground as the pig, whose four legs were moving him as fast as four piglet legs can move (which is surprisingly fast), sped in his direction. At the last moment, right as the pig's corkscrew tail slipped through a big boy's fingers, Clarence reached out and snagged that little pig's back legs with his grit-covered hands.

Uncle Leon's advice saved the day because that pig squirmed, hollered and tried to slip out of Clarence's hands, but Clarence's filthy hands muckled onto him and didn't let go. The announcer said, "Folks, we have a winner!" and the crowd cheered. Uncle Leon let out a hearty "Yahoo!"

But the loudest cheers came from Robby and Ricky, who had come back to watch. They were waving wildly at Clarence, their faces a mixture of surprise and respect.

That evening, after Uncle Leon had brought them all home, Clarence skipped happily over to Leon's workshop, leading Walter (for that's what Clarence named his pig) on a string. Clarence said his silent hello to Geraldine and went to stand beside his uncle, who was busy rebuilding a radio.

"Uncle Leon, how did you know what to do at the pig scramble today?" Clarence asked.

Uncle Leon stopped working and picked up the picture on the windowsill. He looked thoughtfully at it, and then at Clarence. Finally he said, "How do you think Geraldine and I met?"

And Uncle Leon told Clarence a story about another pig scramble, many years ago, when a little boy, smaller than his four brothers, figured out how to let the pig come to him.

About the author

Jessica Kinney is a Maine native and mother of five who lives and writes on the coast of Maine. A Bowdoin College graduate and former middle- and high-school English teacher, Kinney says *The Pig Scramble* was inspired by a true story about her husband, who grew up as the youngest child on a Maine dairy farm and really did win a pig at a local fair. *The Pig Scramble* is her first children's book.

About the illustrator

Sarah S. Brannen is the author and illustrator of *Uncle Bobby's Wedding*. She also illustrated *Mathias Franey, Powder Monkey*; *The ABC Book of American Homes*; and *Digging for Troy: From Homer to Hisarlik*. Forthcoming books include *The Ugly Duckling* (Sterling Publishing, 2013) and *Tooth Truth* (Scholastic Press). For more information, visit www.sarahbrannen.com.

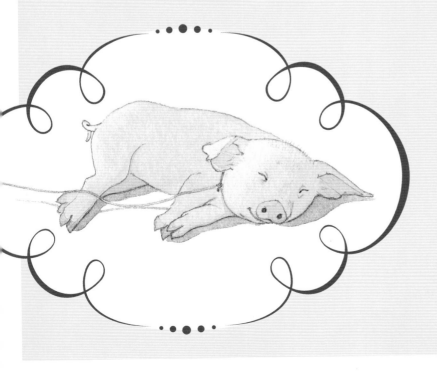

DATE DUE

MY 31 '90	OC 23 '9	JUL 05 '96	
JE 26 '90	NO 27'9	MAY 06 '98	
SE 24 '90	JA 18'9	JY 08 '04	
OC 20 '90	JY 3'9	SE 10'0	
MY 16 '91	JY 21'93	JY 07 '0	
JE 17'91	JY 29'9	DE T 3 '0	
AG 01 '0	MAR 28 '94	JY 05 '10	
AG 8'9	SEP 1 5 '94		
AG 19'91	NOV 8 '94		
SE 4'91	JUL 31 '95		
SE 30'9	NOV 1 6 95		
	DEC 1 1 95		

DEMCO